for
GAYE

Copyright © 2003 by Allan Drummond
Distributed in Canada by Douglas & McIntyre Ltd.
Color separations by Hong Kong Scanner Arts
Printed and bound in the United States of America by Berryville Graphics
First edition, 2003
1 3 5 7 9 10 8 6 4 2

Library of Congress Cataloging-in-Publication Data
Drummond, Allan.
   The flyers / Allan Drummond.— 1st ed.
      p.   cm.
   Summary: In 1903, a group of children on the beach at Kitty Hawk, North Carolina,
dream of flying and witness the first flight of the Wright brothers. Includes a chronology of
milestones in the history of flight.
   ISBN 0-374-32410-7
   1. Wright, Orville, 1871–1948—Juvenile fiction.   2. Wright, Wilbur, 1867–1912—Juvenile
fiction.   [1. Wright, Orville, 1871–1948—Fiction.   2. Wright, Wilbur, 1867–1912—Fiction.
3. Flight—Fiction.]   I. Title.

PZ7.D8247 Fl 2003
[E]—dc21
                                                                              2002026443

THE FLYERS

Allan Drummond

Frances Foster Books • Farrar, Straus and Giroux • New York

When the wind blows in hard from the ocean
we all climb up the sand dunes,
and then we run down,
holding our coattails open,
trying to fly—
and we nearly take off!

We want to be the first people ever in the world
to *fly*!

Just like Orville and Wilbur Wright,
who come down to Kitty Hawk
to fly their crazy kites.

The Wright brothers say they like our sand dunes
and their gentle slopes
and the strong sea breeze.

If I could fly I'd swoop up above the treetops
and look down on my house and the world below
and wave to my mom.

The Wright brothers started by making a big kite
that a man can ride in and control,
and soon they will make a machine
that a man can fly anywhere.

Jamie says if they do that, then one day he will invent
a flying machine big enough to carry *two* people,
and he'll take me for a ride all over Kitty Hawk.

The Wright brothers say that the important thing
is to make a flying machine that they can
take off in, land, control, and steer.
If they can do this, then they could fly *everywhere.*

Josie says one day she'll go *everywhere* in *her* flying machine.
She will go exploring and dare to cross the ocean
and maybe even fly to Africa and scare the elephants and monkeys.

The Wright brothers say that if they can
make an engine powerful enough and light enough
it will carry a heavy flying machine right up into the air
to fly by itself.

Davey says he's not interested in exploring.
He's going to make a *flying war machine*
and fly it right over the Macy gang's hideout
and drop rocks and water bombs on the roof
and give them the fright of their lives.

The Wright brothers say that their newest machine,
the *Flyer*, will make history
if one of them can take off in it and land safely.

Then I thought that if Jamie is going to take *two* people in his machine,
then one day we should *all* build a huge *flying bus*
and carry whole groups of people to visit their families
around the world.

And then little Henry shouted, "If *everyone* is making flying machines,
then *I* will build one that just goes straight up to the *moon*
and I will go for a *moon walk*!"
We all laughed at that idea.

Then one day the Wright brothers were down in Kitty Hawk,
and they pushed the *Flyer* outside for a test run.

They called Mr. Daniels over from the life-saving station.

They showed him how to use a camera
and said he should click when they shouted *"Now!"*

Word got around.
And more lifeguards came over from their lookouts near the ocean.

Then Wilbur held on to the wing of the *Flyer*
and said to everyone,
"Holler and clap and try to cheer Orville when he gets started!"

And then the *Flyer* moved down into the wind,
its engine roared,
and the whole machine took off!
Orville was at the controls
and it really flew!

Wilbur shouted "Now!" and Mr. Daniels snapped his
world-famous photograph.

Everyone cheered!

And that was it!
Orville had controlled the *Flyer* in the air! It was only for twelve seconds,
but it was enough to make history.

They experimented some more,
and at lunchtime Wilbur took the controls
and you should have seen it!
The *Flyer* stayed up in the air for nearly a minute!

The Wright brothers wrote it all down later and said,
"We have demonstrated beyond any reasonable doubt
that the *Flyer* is capable of sustained flight."

I guess history was made that day
because they had built an aircraft that would go wherever they wanted it to.
You could say that they were the first people in the world to really *fly*.

We talk about it a lot
and then *we* go flying

with our coattails open
wherever *we* want.

I fly up over my house . . .

Jamie swoops me up over Kitty Hawk . . .

Josie zooms off to Africa, exploring . . .

Davey takes the controls of his flying war machine . . .

Then we all join hands and make a huge flying bus . . .

and little Henry goes off on a moon walk.